The use of too many [questions should be]
avoided, as it is more [important to]
encourage comment and discussion than
to expect particular answers.

Care has been taken to retain sufficient
realism in the illustrations and subject
matter to enable a young child to have fun
identifying objects, creatures and
situations.

It is wise to remember that patience and
understanding are very important, and that
children do not all develop evenly or
at the same rate. Parents should not be
anxious if children do not give correct
answers to those questions that are asked.
With help, they will do so in their own time.

The brief notes at the
back of this book will
enable interested parents
to make the fullest use
of these **Ladybird
talkabout** books.

Ladybird Books Loughborough

In addition to its main purpose of increasing any young child's vocabulary and understanding, this book will be especially useful in a family where a new baby is expected or has recently arrived.

Talking about the illustrations, and showing how an older child can be helpful and involved in the new situation, will provide reassurance that he or she is still just as important a member of the family – and as much loved as ever. In this way, the resentment and jealousy that often occurs can be avoided.

compiled by Ethel Wingfield

illustrated by Harry Wingfield

The publishers wish to acknowledge the assistance of the nursery school advisers who helped with the preparation of this book, especially that of Lady Britton, Chairman, and Miss M Puddephat, M Ed, Vice Chairman of The British Association for Early Childhood Education (formerly The Nursery School Association).

talkabout
baby

Getting ready
for baby

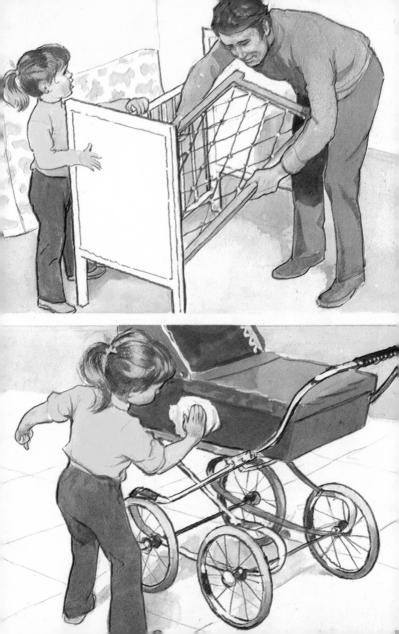

Talk about mommy coming home with

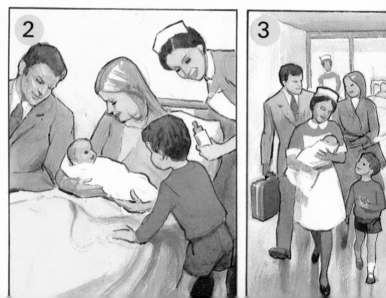

the new baby

LOOK and find
another like this

and this

and this

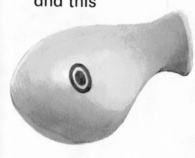

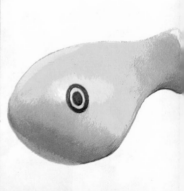

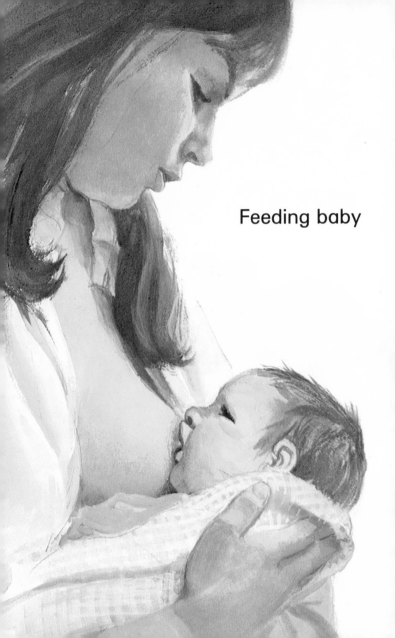

Feeding baby

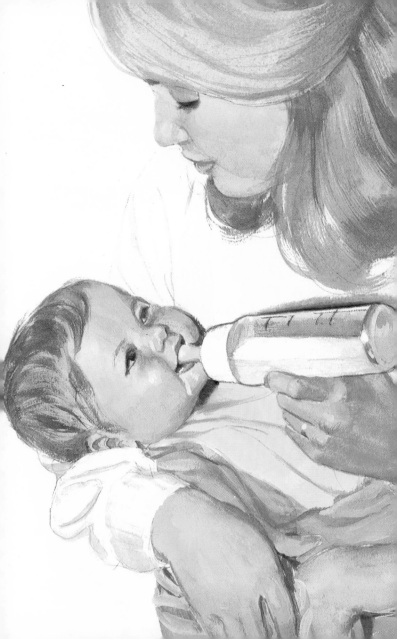

Which of these
should baby have?

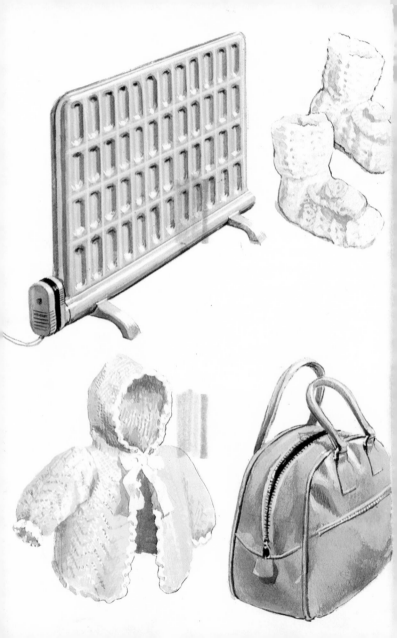

Which help to
keep baby warm?

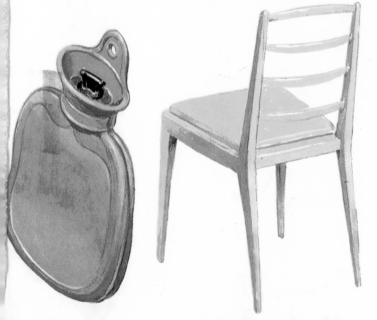

What is happening here?

LOOK and find
another like this

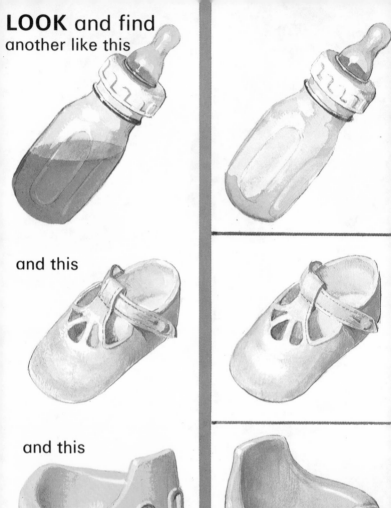

and this

and this

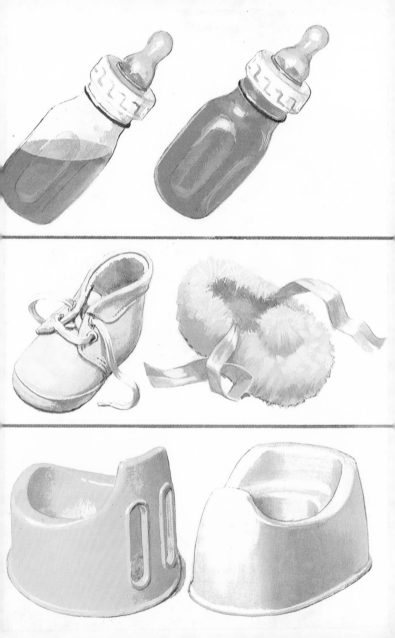

Helping

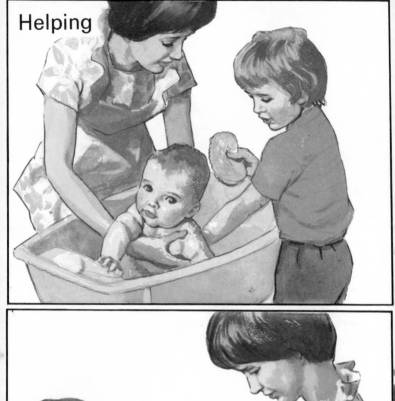

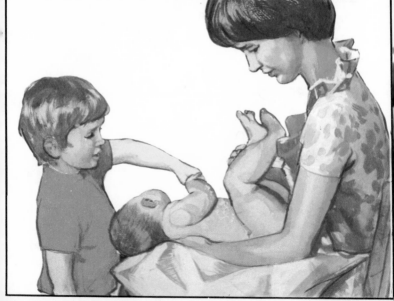

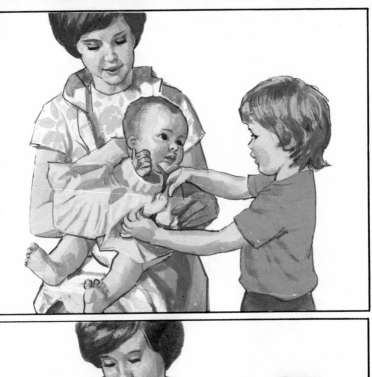

Which go together?

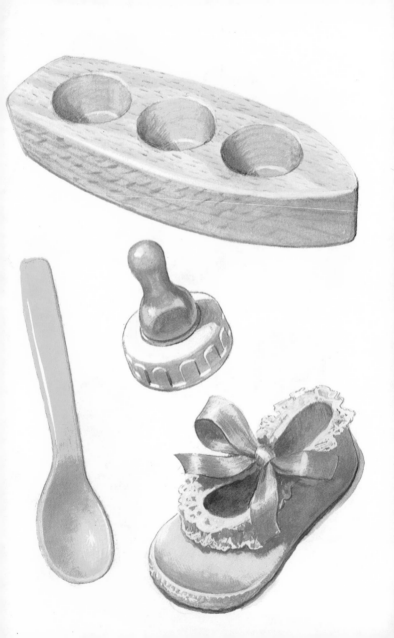

Talk about the twins

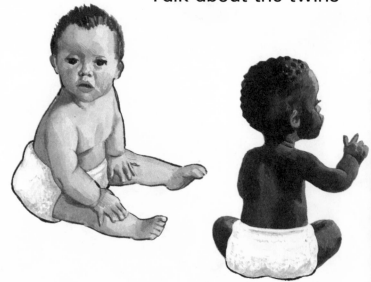

Tell the story

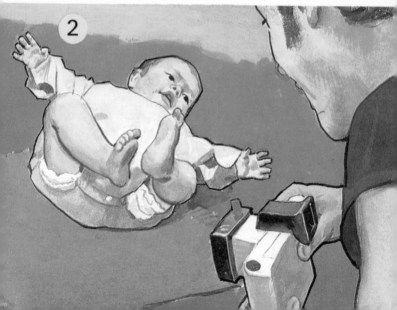

Which are safe for
baby to play with?

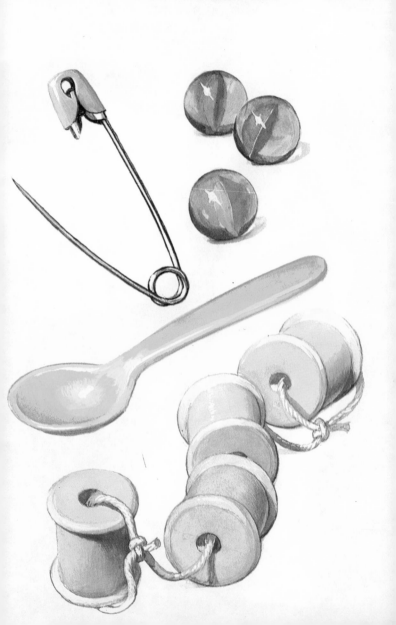

Tell the story

1

2

Count the babies

Count the baby carriage beads
and talk about the colors

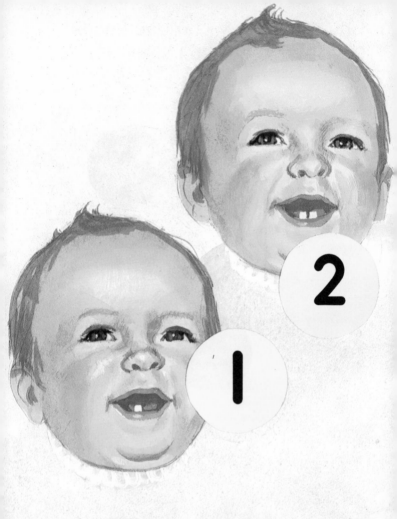

How many teeth?

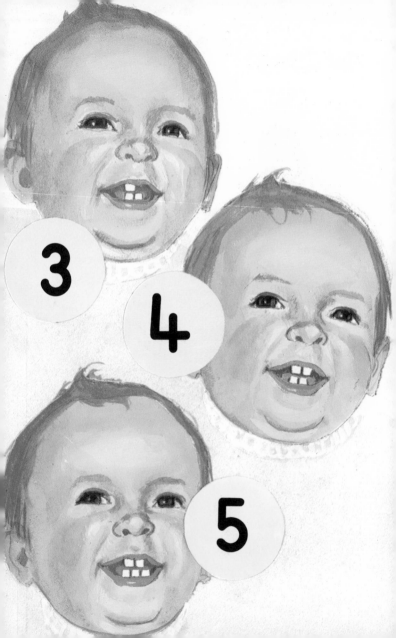

Which would we buy
for a baby?

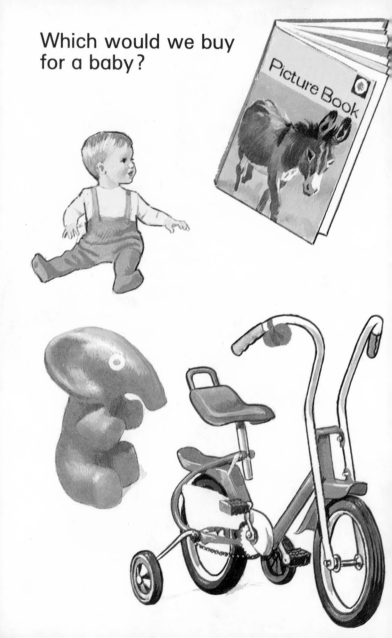

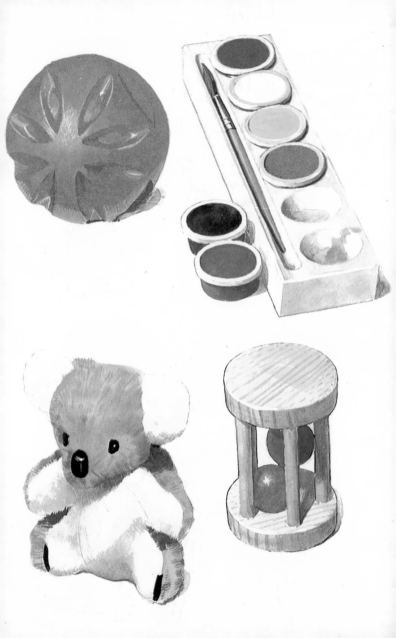

What are they for ?

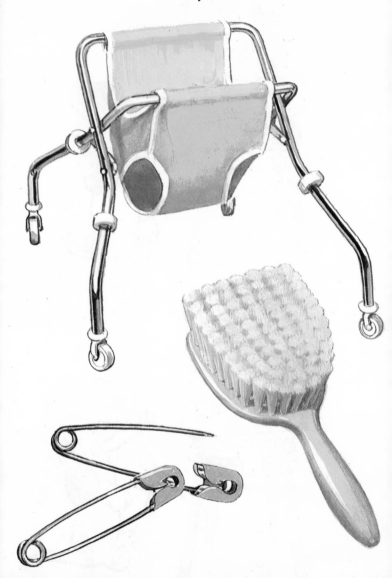

Match each picture
with its black shape

Playing with baby

Tell the story

1

2

Suggestions for extending the use of this **talkabout** book . . .

The illustrations have been planned to help increase a child's vocabulary and understanding, and the page headings are only brief suggestions as to how these illustrations can be used. At some time every child becomes aware of the arrival of a new baby, if not in his own home then in that of a friend or relative. You could therefore talk about the necessary preparations before a baby arrives, and how helpful an older child can be even at that early stage. You could also talk about the temporary absence of the mother while she is in the hospital, how babies are fed, what happens on a visit to the clinic, and so on.

There are numerous opportunities for discussion on the use of the various articles shown, how they are used and where they may be found in a child's home. A child can be helped to understand important concepts such as (in the hospital illustrations) the nurse's